TAKE MINE!

MY YOUNG DAYS.

BY THE
AUTHOR OF "EVENING AMUSEMENT," "LETTERS EVERYWHERE,"

ILLUSTRATIONS BY
PAUL KONEWKA

My Young Days

Copyright © 2010 by Indo-European Publishing

For information and contact visit our website at:
IndoEuropeanPublishing.com

The present edition is a revised version of an earlier publication of this work, produced in the current edition with completely new, easy to read format, and is set and proofread by Alfred Aghajanian for Indo-European Publishing.

Cover Design by Indo-European Design Team

ISBN: 978-1-60444-271-7

IndoEuropean
Publishing.com
Los Angeles, CA, USA

Contents

1

HOME SICKNESS

"I want to go home!"

How many times in my life, I wonder, have these words come rushing up from the very bottom of my heart, tumbling everything out of the way, never listening to reason, never stopping for thought? How many times since that dreary afternoon in the great, big drawing-room at grandmamma's? And, oh dear me! what miserable heartache comes before that fearful want! Oh, grown-up people, don't you know how sour everything tastes, and how yellow everything looks, and how sick everything makes one, when one wants to go home?

So it was that one wretched day. How well I remember it all! The large, large drawing-room so full of cushions, couches, easy-chairs, little tables covered with funny knick-knacks, marble-slabs and more knick-knacks, beautiful fire-screens, large mirrors, soft fur lying about on the floor, and many-coloured antimacassars on the chairs. By and by, all these wonders had happy memories pinned on to them, of uproarious games with merry little play-fellows. Now, I was all alone, and very lonely, in it all. True, there was grandmamma nodding in her easy-chair, in the firelight, on one side, and there was Uncle Hugh reading the "Times" by the same light on the other. But what were either of them to the little tired stranger on the low stool between them? Once grandmamma's eyes had opened just to look at me, and say, "Making pretty pictures of the red coals, my dearie?"

And Uncle Hugh had answered, "Yes, to be sure; dreaming of the King of Salamanders!"

And they went to sleep again or went on reading, and the little company smile faded away from my face, and I went back to those very real dreams of the nursery at home, and baby there, and little brother, and papa and mamma, and the long time ago, hours and hours ago! when I said good-bye, and Bobbie kissed his hand out of window, and the carriage took me off—a happy little woman, really going in the puff-puff! Oh, how could I ever have felt so happy then and be so miserable now? Had I ever thought that I was coming away from them all, with nobody at all but Jane, the new nursemaid, to take care of me? Had I ever thought how *quite* alone I should be, never able to find my way in this great, big house, sure to get lost in some of the passages? And how could I ever go to sleep without Bobbie close by, and wouldn't Bobbie cry for me at home? And oh, nurse wouldn't be there to tuck me up, and perhaps grandmamma wouldn't like the candle left! And who would give me my good-night kiss like,—like,—oh, oh, like— But it would come, that great big sob, it wasn't any use to choke it back! And, when it had come, of course, it was all over with me, and there was nothing for it but to cry out just as if I was not in that grand drawing-room—

"I want to go home! I want, oh, I do want mamma!"

What a disturbance that cry of mine did make, to be sure! Grandmamma was wide-awake in a moment, looking very much distressed, and laying her hand on the bell. This troubled me very much; for hadn't Jane told me when she brushed my hair and made me tidy, that I was to go down and be a good girl, "and do things pretty" in the drawing-room, and would she scold me if I was sent away for crying and making a noise? But Uncle Hugh came to my rescue, threw away his paper, and cuddled me up in his great strong arms almost like papa. And he showed me his watch, and made it strike, and then began to show me all kinds of wonders about the room: little tiny black men under a glass case, small china monkeys, cats and frogs, and funny shells and fishes, and snakes' skins, and lots of other things. And after that we came back to the easy-chair, and he sang me sailors' songs, and told me all about "The House that Jack built!"

"Little woman," he said at last, "did you ever hear of 'The Goose that Jack killed?'" and then he sang in his funny way, "This is the goose that Jack killed; and this is the cat that wanted the goose that Jack killed; and this is the dog that chased the cat that wanted the goose that Jack killed; and this is the thief that cheated the dog that chased the cat that wanted the goose that Jack killed; and this is the dream that haunted the thief that cheated the dog that chased the cat that wanted the goose that Jack killed; and this"—

But "Good night, Uncle Hugh, there's Jane come to fetch Miss Sissy to her tea, upstairs in the nursery."

THE CAT THAT WANTED THE GOOSE

2

UNCLE HUGH'S STORY

Yes, tea alone in the nursery, that strange room that looked as if it hadn't been a nursery for a great many years, and was as queer and awkward as an old woman trying to look young again. No clatter of spoons to make baby laugh, no chatter of childish voices, only little me, all alone with Jane—little me, so puzzled and strange and bewildered in the new place! Perhaps Jane thought me dull, for she talked away fast enough, about that dear old lady, my grandmamma, and about the beautiful place we were in, and what if Master Bobbie should grow up some day to find it all his own, and be the lord of it all. I didn't care much if he did; I only wanted him now, little boy as he was, to put his fat arms round my neck, for I was "little sister" to nobody here; it was mere mockery calling me "Miss Sissy" all the time. Perhaps Jane heard the sigh, for she stopped afterwards in the middle of her long story about the little cousins from over the sea, that were coming here in a day or two. She had me on her lap, and she was just taking off my shoes and socks, but she drew my head to her shoulder, and told me that I had "Janie-panie" with me, who was always going to take care of me all the time. I was very tired, and my eyes went shut on the pillow after that, before they had time to cry home-sick tears. And next day there were so many new things to see; two little puppies to make friends with, beside the parrot and pussy.

But I mustn't begin to tell you all the things that happened that day. You see, I have made quite a long story of my first evening, so you must try and fancy all about the walk in the park with Jane, and the drive with Grandmamma to the town, and the toy-shop, and what we bought there.

When we came home it was my tea-time; and after that Jane changed my frock, and did my hair, and took me down to dessert, in the dining-room. Ah, then the shy fit came on, and I bent my head very gravely to take the sweet bits off Uncle Hugh's fork, I remember. But when he had pushed back his chair, given his arm to grandmamma, and his hand to me, and taken us into the drawing-room—then, while he made me nestle down on his knee in the soft easy-chair, all my shyness went away at the look of his merry eyes.

"Now for the goose that Jack killed," he said; and then and there began the funniest story you ever heard. Only I can't tell it in the funny words and with the merry, twinkling glances he gave me.

It was when Uncle Hugh was a middy, and he had been sailing in a great big ship ever so long, till at last they came to some foreign country, I don't know where. Well, Uncle Hugh and his friend Jack Miller went roaming about, very glad to get off the sea. They took possession of a little empty hut on the beach, and

THE DOG THAT CHASED THE CAT

spent some of the time there, and some of the time roaming about on the hills. Now it chanced, one day, that they saw a flock of wild geese flying over the shore. Jack had a gun with him, and he instantly shot one of these geese. Uncle Hugh says they had had so much salt meat at sea, that they smacked their lips to think of a nice fat goose for dinner. So they carried it off to their hut, and then they pulled off all the feathers one by one, and made it quite ready to cook. What funny cooks they must have been! But it wasn't quite time to roast it, so they tied it up by a string to the door and went away, leaving the captain's dog, Neptune, to watch it.

Now, Nep was a very funny dog—a nervous dog, Uncle Hugh called him—and he was quite afraid something would happen. By and by, poor pussy came to have a peep at the goosey-gander, and she climbed up the steps on tip-toe just to look. Nep watched her, and didn't feel easy in his mind, and when poor pussy just stretched forward her head (because she was a little short-sighted, I dare say), Nep could bear it no longer.

THE THIEF THAT STOLE THE GOOSE

He gave a great loud bark, and flew along the road after the wretched, flying cat. Silly dog! while he was gone after puss, and just as he had his fore-paws quite over her back, up comes a sly thief to the hut door, quietly unhooks the bird, and runs off the other way, with its head hanging over his shoulder. "And, so, you see, Sissy," said Uncle Hugh in his funnily grave way, "poor Jack and I came back to find our dinner all gone!" But they got scent of the thief, and they caught him and shut him up in their little hut, and locked him in, and left him with nothing but bread and water. "For there was no policeman there, Sissy; we had to play policemen ourselves."

THE DREAM THAT HAUNTED THE THIEF

And there they left him all night. And the poor thief thought about his little hungry children at home, till he fell asleep and dreamt (I wonder how Uncle Hugh knew that?) that he saw the goose all smoking hot, gravy and all, and a knife and fork all ready to cut it up.

But they didn't mean to be cruel—I don't believe Uncle Hugh could be! So they had a nice, hot supper themselves on board the big ship, and plenty of fun, and lots of merry songs. And then they cut three big slices and put them aside.

And don't you think the thief-man must have been surprised when he saw the nice breakfast that Jack brought him next morning? I think Uncle Hugh said that he wrapped it all up and took it home to his children. How queer he must have felt as he slunk off, the sailors standing round and giving him three cheers and plenty of jokes!

3

THE LITTLE STOWAWAY

One of my earliest friends at the Park was a little French boy, a kind of page of my uncle's. Shall I tell you about him? You will think it very funny that a servant-boy should be allowed to be my friend, so I must explain.

Little Gus, as my uncle called him—though his real name was Gustave—was altogether a little foreigner. He couldn't talk English at all properly; in fact, the greater part of our conversation was carried on by signs. He was very much afraid of everybody in the house, except Uncle Hugh. He thought there was nobody in all the world like the Captain, as he called him. His bright eyes used to twinkle and his white teeth shine whenever he could find a chance of running an errand, or doing any little job for the Captain; and I think it was, perhaps, because he took me for the Captain's little pet that he grew so fond of me.

He would follow me all about the garden, and watch

me as I talked away to Jane, and be ready to find my ball or fetch my hoop the minute I wanted them.

Now, after we had been a little while at the Park, I found that Jane had got very fond of flowers, and was always anxious to go to the glass-houses directly we came out into the garden.

"Why, Miss Sissy," she would say, "there never was anything like the ferns, and the orange-trees, and the cactuses in them houses; and Mr. Owen so civil-like in showing them to us, too."

So off we went to the hot-houses, and there Mr. Owen and Jane talked and talked till I got tired of the hot air, and went to play outside; and there just outside was Gus, always waiting to pick me the prettiest flowers, and find me the first sweet violets. But I was shy, and his words were so foreign that they frightened me; nor did I like at all being called "Petite mademoiselle," which was not my name, and couldn't mean anything that I could think of. At last I grew braver, and one day I ventured to ask—

"Who is your papa?"

"Me hab no papa, no mamma!" he said, looking very full at me.

"Where do you live then?" I asked. "You're not a bit like Bobbie!"

"Me live wid de Capitaine; me never will leaf de Capitaine—never, never, never!" he answered eagerly.

This made me feel very queer, and I think I looked half-frightened, for his look changed quickly, and he said, smiling his own sunny smile—

"Me fetch petite mademoiselle somet'ing nice; me fetch de puss dat de Capitaine just bring home!"

A pussy! That sounded pleasant, and I waited eagerly for his return. I waited a long time, as it seemed, and I had grown tired, and was looking for daisies on the grass, when I heard his step and the tap of his favourite holly-stick on the gravel. What a funny boy he was to call that "something nice"!

There he stood, his eyes and mouth all one smile, and held out at arm's length by the ears a dead rabbit. My look and exclamation of horror made him grave at once.

POOR DEAD PUSSY!

"Oh, the poor little rabbit!" I cried. "Has Uncle Hugh killed him quite dead?"

"Yes, yes, he quite dead! De Capitaine's gun kill him quite, de small dog pick him up. Petite mademoiselle not frighten, he quite dead!"

Ah, that was just the reason of my fright! Away I ran to Jane, and hid my face in her gown; and a very vigorous scolding did she give the French boy when she found what he had done.

Poor fellow! he was very much disconcerted, and did not know what to say. Two hours after he came back, and finding me alone just going for a drive, he said softly—

"Little puss all alive now, run away in de voods. Petite mademoiselle, come see?"

What did he mean? The rabbit could not be "quite dead" at one time, and "all alive" afterwards. But grandmamma was coming downstairs, and I had no time to answer him. By and by, when I was lying back on the soft cushions stroking grandmamma's pretty white fur, I told her all my puzzle.

"Ah, my pet," she said, "poor Gus had a very cruel French father, and doesn't know any better. He ran away from home when your uncle's ship was touching at Marseilles, and hid himself in the hold. They found him when they got out to sea—a little stowaway the sailors called him—and your uncle liked his dark, pitiful eyes, and was very kind to him; but he has not learnt much yet that's good. Don't have too much to say to him, my darling!"

Well, it wasn't very likely I should, for he and I found it not very easy to understand each other; yet he liked to do anything he could for me, and was always watching to see what I wanted.

Nearly a year after that, I remember, it was very cold, and the little southern boy felt it especially. He had grown ever so tall and thin, but not strong, and he went about looking blue and shivery. How I came to be still at the Park I will tell you in another place, but there I was, and my friend Gus won my pity by his wretched looks. I used to look at his blue hands, and wonder what could be done. At last I remembered a pair of warm knitted gloves, that had been given me, which I never wore. They had no fingers, only a thumb, and I doubted whether Gus would wear them; but I made up my mind that he would be glad anyhow to keep his chilblains from the wind.

I don't think I shall ever forget his look when I presented them to him, holding them by the pretty blue wool which fastened them together. That his "petite mademoiselle" should think of him, and make him a present, too! and then that that present should be one that he could not anyhow use! It was fairly too much for him; he looked at them, he looked at me, turned furiously red, stammered, stuttered, turned round, and literally ran away!

I never tried to make him a second present.

4

MY HOME, AND WHAT IT WAS LIKE

Now, do you know, I feel rather ashamed of myself that I have not all this while told you in the least who I was, or where I came from. I began in the middle by saying, "I want to go home," but never told you in the least where my home was, nor what it was.

Well, to tell you the truth, I did not know much about my family history in those early days. I knew that my name was Mary Emily Marshall, commonly called Sissy, and I knew that my papa was "the gentleman that makes all the sick people well,"—"or tries to," Jane would add. I never did. Of course, if my papa tried to do anything he did it. That was my doctrine. We lived quite down in the country among the poor people, and we were not rich ourselves. Mamma had been born in this beautiful park, and I know now, though I did not then, that it was a great trouble at the Park when she married the country doctor, who loved the poor people so much that he would not leave them to grow rich and honoured as a London physician. But there was no grandpapa left now to be angry; and grandmamma, though we had never seen her, we had always loved for the beautiful presents she sent us.

There were only three of us at this time—my little self; Bobbie, a boy of four years old, boasting of the fattest, rosiest cheeks in the world; and wee Willie, the white-faced, fretful baby of six months. Oh, how well I remember the old house, with its great lamp hanging out over the lonely road, and shining among the trees, to show the villagers the way up to their good, kind friend the doctor. Many were the blessings we little ones used to get as we passed down the village street, and we owed them all to our father's goodness.

Happy times we had of it, Bobbie and I, in that old house at the top of the hill. I don't think any little brothers and sisters were ever quite such good friends. There were three years between us, but I was little and he was big, so nobody guessed it, and we played together, and never thought which was the elder. The great treat of the day was the game with papa in the evening, but that couldn't be counted upon. Very often he would have to leave the dinner-table suddenly, and when we heard his peculiar slam of the hall-door before the bell rang to summon us down, we knew that we had lost our game, and we comforted ourselves by telling each other that papa had gone to see some little sick child like baby Willie, and to make him quite well; and then we would make up our minds to a good quiet game by ourselves.

We used to take turns, he playing at doll with me one time, and I playing at horses with him next time. How

PAPA AND MAMMA

well I remember my hairless, eyeless doll, and all the pleasure she gave us! And good-natured old nurse was quite willing, whenever Willie was a little better than usual, to work wonders with dolly's toilet. One week she would be a fine, grand lady, to whom Bobby would act footman and I lady's-maid. Next week, she was a soldier fighting grand battles, and lying dead on the battle-field at last, with a patch of red paint on the forehead, and we two singing dirges and songs of victory; and then, all of a sudden, the soldier was turned into a baby, with long white clothes and the prettiest of caps.

The day that grandmamma's letter came, asking for "one of the dear children to stay with her," dolly was just learning to walk. We were having our firelight play before tea. I had tied up my curls to look like a grown woman's hair, and I had papa's umbrella to keep the rain off dolly in her first walk. Bobbie had papa's hat and stick, and he held Rosalinda's other hand. I was just telling him not to walk so fast, because his long strides would tire our little girl, when I heard papa's voice calling me.

In a minute more I was standing between his knees, and mamma was watching my face as I tried to take in the idea of this first visit.

"Jane shall go with you, my darling—you will not be all alone," said mamma; "indeed, you shall not go at all if you had rather not, but grandmamma wants to have you."

And then papa added a great deal about seeing the place where mamma lived when she was my age, and told me that I should come back with such rosy cheeks. And all the while I was thinking of the new doll's-house that grandmamma would give me perhaps. The thought of this took me back to Rosalinda, and I felt sure that Bobbie would let her fall if I didn't be quick and go to him. So I said, "Yes, I will go," very much in a hurry, and was ever so glad to get away and run upstairs again.

"Queer little fish!" I heard papa say as I left the room. "She thinks a great deal more about the doll and Bobbie, than of the visit to Beecham."

"Children never look far forward," was mamma's answer.

But I did look forward by and by. When dear Rosalinda was safely tucked up in her cradle, and Bobbie and I had "time to think," as we said, then we talked it all over. And very wonderful plans we made. Such numbers of injunctions did I lay upon Bobbie, as to the care of the dolls while I was away, that the poor little fellow said with a sigh, "Yes, I'll try and 'member, Sissy!"

So I consoled him by the thought of all the presents grandmamma would send him when I came back. In fact, I was to bring something for everybody, so I thought. Two dear little rabbits for Bobbie, perhaps a new black silk gown for nurse, a beautiful sash for the baby, and so on, and so on.

SO NICE!

The next afternoon Bobbie and I had our last feast. Do *you* often have feasts? I don't mean cake and fruit, and good things at the dinner-table. Oh no, I mean a real tiny feast all to yourselves, with the nursery-chair unscrewed to make table and chair, with square paper plates twisted at the corners, paper dishes with sugar on one, currants on another, rice or raisins on another, and little doll's-house cups for the make-believe wine and the real milk. Ah, that nice sugared milk taken in little sips out of the oldest nursery-spoons! How well I can fancy myself now, giving Bobbie his spoonful, while pussy looked enviously up at us? Then it was that the bright thought struck me that I would bring home some real Beecham kittens to puss, that would do quite well in the place of those dear little lost ones, that James had taken away and forgotten ever to bring back? Well, you know, all the preparations were made, my pretty new frock tried on, all my kisses given, and all sorts of messages sent home from the station, and in the highest of spirits my first start in life was accomplished. What my feelings were when the day came to an end, you know, so I need not tell you.

5

LITTLE COUSINS

So now you know who I was, where I came from, and all about me. Let me, then, go on telling you about this remarkable visit to grandmamma. You have heard all about those first quiet days, when I was all alone, the only little thing in all the place. It was very different afterwards, I can tell you.

You know Jane had told me all that was going to happen. Indeed, she talked always very fast, and didn't mind filling my little head with her opinions of my betters which was certainly a mistake. It was a shame, she said, that my uncle, "the Reverend," should send all his children here, while he and his wife went taking their travels and their pleasure all about to those gay foreign places!

Grandmamma talked about it in quite a different way. She told me how ill my aunt had been, so ill that my uncle had been obliged to take her away from England for the whole winter. And she said that now they had left the place on the beautiful Swiss lake, and were going to try some German baths. Only they could not take the children there, so they were to come and stay at the Park for a month or too, the while.

I thought this would be very nice, and I began to ask all sorts of questions about Harry and Lottie, and Alick and Murray, and Bertie and the baby. How funny it would seem when the nursery was so full! I thought the day would never come. But it did. The carriage was sent off to the station, and in due time it came back, quite full to overflowing with children!

There was a good deal of shyness at first, when we all stood in a row, and looked at each other, answering grandmamma's questions seriously, and feeling very odd. But that was only the first evening. Next day we were quite happy and comfortable, had a very merry breakfast, and then a delightful ramble about the gardens and orchards. Of course, I was only one of the little ones, coming in between Alick and Murray, feeling very small beside Lottie and Harry. Yet we were all very good friends, and Lottie soon told me that she thought it would be very nice to have a girl to talk to, and not only boys. This remark pleased me, though when I thought of Bobbie, it sounded rather strange. Indeed, I am not sure that I was not a little too fond of boys' play.

I remember feeling rather disappointed one day when she said to me in the garden—

"Sissy, let's come and have a nice quiet walk together, and leave the boys to play by themselves."

Now, three of the boys were just preparing for a military march, one with a bright flag, another with a trumpet, and another with a sword-stick, so-called; and there was a most refreshing prospect of shouting, stamping, and huzzahs! Do you wonder that I turned away rather unwillingly?

GOING TO THE WARS

However, Lottie's confidences soon made up for it all. Such beautiful stories Lottie could tell! When she began to talk about the Alps, and the blue lake and the mountain flowers, I thought it seemed almost as good as my hymns and verses. I know I looked up at her with eyes full of admiration, and when she put her arms round me, and gave me a loving kiss, I thought I had never been so happy before.

And then she listened to all I had to tell her about

Bobbie, and baby Willie, and Rosalinda, and gave me her advice about dressing Rosalinda like the Queen.

My letters, too, she read, and said they were very nice, which made me love mamma for writing them all the more. And she showed me her own letter that had just come across the sea, with its foreign stamps and thin paper. Quite a nice talk it was altogether, and we were ever so sorry when we were called in to dinner.

My boy-cousins were very polite to me at first, and hardly seemed to know what to make of me. Harry was a little too patronizing, called me "a mite of a thing," and played tricks upon me in a gentle way. But then he was not often with us. He had not been a night in the house before he had quite determined to be a sailor like Uncle Hugh, so it followed, as a matter of course, that he must be always with him.

Force of habit, however, made him confide all his plans and thoughts to Lottie, so that our private talks in the shrubbery were often interrupted by his merry voice. Then he would throw himself down among the grass and periwinkles, and tell us all about his future ship. This usually ended in Lottie's being carried off to make sails or flags for his new craft. Then, being left to myself, I soon ran off to my other cousins, nothing loath to have a game of romps with them.

Alick seemed likely to be my special friend. What a funny little fellow he must have been, though I did not think so then! Jane called him a little dandy, much to his displeasure; yet I am afraid his friendship was likely to increase my childish vanity. He was so fond of decking me with flowers, making wreaths for me, and then looking at me, and sometimes comparing my hair or eyes with Lottie's; and his look of vexation if my face was dirty or my pinafore torn, often comes back to me even now when I feel untidy in any way.

One afternoon, when Alick and I and one of the other boys were alone, it suddenly came into our wise little heads that we would play at going to a party. What vast preparations we made! What pains the boys took to tie up my sleeves with some bright ribbon meant for Harry's flags! How cleverly we succeeded in carrying off a hair-brush, and what a long time it took to decide how the boys' hair and ties should be arranged! And then came the flowers, my wreath, and the bouquet to be carried for me by one of my gentlemen.

We were all ready, I remember, and I was just taking Alick's arm, and we had all put on our best airs and graces for a solemn entrance to the supposed ball-room, when, all of a sudden, who should come round the corner but Uncle Hugh and Harry!

Oh, those bursts of laughter pealing out again and again! Oh, the writhings and twistings of Uncle Hugh in his excessive mirth! Would they *ever* stop laughing? Even now my cheeks almost tingle with those painful blushes, and my heart beats with that frightened shame!

And yet it was for Alick that I was chiefly troubled, as I saw him fling down the flowers and run, while

Harry, shouting "conceited young jackanapes," pursued him at full speed. I had never seen such rough play or heard such mocking laughter, and I burst into tears, sobbing out my trouble on my uncle's shoulder as he carried me off and laughingly soothed me, pressing the prickly wreath all the while against my head.

GOING TO A PARTY

It was a long time before our adventure was forgotten. Harry's merry jokes brought the colour over and over again to my face, and the angry words to Alick's lips. But we were both cured, certainly, for the time, of any love of display or dandyism!

6

WHAT ABOUT LESSONS?

And now, little reader, I know quite well what thought has been popping in and out of your head all this time. You have been wanting to ask me what had become of lessons all these weeks, and how a number of little boys and girls could be allowed to run wild, doing just what they liked all day long.

Well, it does seem very shocking, and there is no denying that, for a whole month, we did not often see the inside of a book. Yet, I had learnt to read, and had been in the habit of learning to spell and to count every day of my life at home. I don't quite know how it came about that we were not all of us a very untamed set after a month's idleness at the Park. Perhaps, it was a good thing for us that grandmamma was what she was. The very perfection of tender kindness we all felt her, and yet there was a certain dignity about her, that made it a simple impossibility to be rough or rude before her. And on the whole we were a great deal with her. When not with her, we were supposed to be picking up a great deal of French from my cousin's Swiss nurse. And so, in our way, we did, although I think Susette learned English a great deal faster than we learned French. Yet, when we wished to coax her, the French words came fast enough, such as they were.

BABY, DEAR!

But I am afraid grandmamma did not think that we were learning quite enough, for one day she called Lottie and me, and told us that she had just seen such a nice young lady, and that she had promised to come and be our governess. What an excitement this news caused us all! How we talked it over all day long. We had many different ideas as to what she was to be like; in fact, the elder boys made pictures of her, which, as it turned out, were anything but good portraits.

How we did look at her that first evening! She was very young, very fair and in deep mourning. That is my earliest impression of her. We had a kind of unconfessed idea that she did not take half pains enough to make us like her. She did not seem to care whether we did or not—hardly, I fancy, to think about the matter. It was just the very end of April, almost the bright May-time, and grandmamma went round the garden with her, Lottie and I making our remarks from a distance. I think we were a little surprised to see our new governess so much at her ease, laughing merrily and talking away to grandmamma, just as if there were no little critics taking note of all. By and by, she came in and sat down in "the schoolroom"— such a new word that seemed!—to write a letter. Lottie and I pretended to be very busy with our dolls in one corner, but we were keeping up our watch, and every now and then we met her eye with a merry twinkle in it, looking greatly amused at us.

"She looks so young, only a girl! she will never be able to manage us, Jane says," Lottie remarked very softly to me; "but then, I daresay, she can be cross enough when she likes, governesses always are!"

All of a sudden, a merry laugh startled us both, and in another minute Lottie found herself flat on the floor, being tickled and kissed and laughed over all at once. I don't think she quite liked it, though she couldn't help laughing, too, but her cheeks were very red, when

Miss Grant raised her own head. She kept Lottie flat on her back, and looked down at her, the most thorough amusement all over her face.

"Cross enough, do you think? Oh, yes, to be sure I can! Cross enough to eat you up at one mouthful, and little Sissy after you!"

How funny it sounded! Lottie laughed and so did I, only very nervously. Then all at once Miss Grant grew very comically grave, and asked us whether we thought we should soon make her cross? And then followed such a funny talk, I think I shall never forget it. Miss Grant was half lying on the sofa now, Lottie and I were bobbing up and down beside her, sometimes looking right into her blue laughing eyes, sometimes hiding our own rosy faces, that she mightn't see how queer she made us feel.

"You don't much like the idea of having a governess, I see," she said; "you fancy it will be lessons, lessons all day long now, a great deal of crying, and punishments, very hard things to learn, and no fun any more. If that's what it really is going to be, I shall get so unhappy that I shall soon run away home again! And then you think I shall have to grow cross and ill-tempered, too—that is the worst part of it all."

She pretended to be ready to cry, and Lottie, who didn't quite like to give up her own opinion, muttered something about "She thought they always were!"

"Are they?" asked Miss Grant, just as if she really wanted to know, and, when we laughed and hid our faces, she went on: "I think I know how it is. This is what you will do to me: You will begin by getting into all the mischief you can think of, and that will give me a headache; and then you will be cross and rude, and that will give me great, deep lines in the forehead; and last of all, you will do vulgar things, that will make my mouth get into the 'don't' shape, which is so ugly, you know; and, by and by, when I look at myself in the glass, I shall find myself turned into a grey-headed old woman, and I shall say, 'Sissy gave me those wrinkles between my eyes, I always had to frown at her so;' and then, 'Those ugly lines by my mouth came when Lottie vexed me so.' What a funny thing it will be to have to remember you in that way when you are grown-up people!"

Of course, we did not like this way of taking it for granted that we were rude, troublesome children, yet there was a funny look in Miss Grant's eyes that seemed as if she didn't really mean what she said. And the end of it all was that we made a compact, as she called it, that we would be ever so good-tempered, and then she and we would have the happiest time together that you can fancy.

And I think it all came true. Thanks to our papas and mammas, we were not quite the rude children we might have been. They had saved us ever so much trouble, and ever so many tears, by teaching us that hardest lesson "do as you are told," before we were old enough to understand its difficulty. And Miss Grant was always so bright and happy that she scarcely ever let us suspect, even in the naughtiest times, that we were "making the lines come." Out of doors she was the merriest among us, and grandmamma would often say to Lottie that she was ever so much older than Miss Grant, because she would walk soberly about with a book, while Miss Grant was having all sorts of fun with the boys. At last she, too, caught the infection, and then we all had the merriest romps together! How well I remember those early summer days, and the luxury of flowers everywhere. Is there anything so happy-looking, so full of overflowing delight, as the long grass, and the buttercups and daisies, hawthorn and bluebells? We thought ourselves very wise about flowers then, and had very decided opinions on the proper blending of colours. Miss Grant was teaching us this, and even now, when I see any one making a nosegay of wild-flowers, I fancy myself running up to her with a handful of bright things, to watch in my eagerness how they were in a minute turned into the beautiful bouquet that nobody could equal or copy.

She had been with us some time, when one morning we had a visitor come to spend the day at Beecham. This lady was not old, yet she had the most wrinkled, aged face I ever saw. When she was gone, Harry, who never minded what he said, asked grandmamma about her, and cried out in surprise when he heard that she had been his own father's playfellow.

"You think Mrs. Mowbray looks double as old as papa, do you?" said grandmamma. "Ah, it is trouble that has aged her. You would not wonder at all those lines and wrinkles if you knew all the sorrow and grief her own poor boys have given her through their sin and wilfulness!"

Lottie and I looked at each other, and then glanced slily at Miss Grant, but I don't think she noticed us. When we were alone again, we resolved that we would try ever so hard to be good.

"Because, you know, Sissy, it wouldn't be nice if Miss Grant were to get her face all puckered and creasy like that, just as if it wanted ironing out, as Susette did with my frock when Murray scrunched it all up under his pillow to hide it. But I suppose you couldn't iron out your face!"

Anyhow, I agreed with Lottie not to run any risks, and I do not think we did. At least, all my memories of that happy year at Beecham are mingled with the bright, merry, gentle friend who made easy all the lessons that could be easy, and gave me courage for those that *had* to be hard; and against whose shoulder I loved to nestle, and listen to Bible-stories with those little hints in them which always set me thinking of my own faults and duties, and made me long to do right, and be the good little Christian girl she wished me to be.

Little reader, dear, are you making lines on anybody's forehead?

7

HURRAH FOR THE HOLIDAYS!

And yet, however pleasant lessons might be, there is no doubt that holidays were pleasant things, too. Saturday afternoons were always welcome, and all the weeks through we were planning what we would do when they came. Of course these plans were sometimes upset by a rainy day; but, even then, what with battledore and shuttlecock, painting and spinning tops, we contrived to make out the time very happily.

And before us all the while was the bright, pleasant prospect of the long summer holidays.

Every now and then during these happy months the thought of home came across me, and sometimes one of mamma's letters would have in it so much about Bobby and his play, and his prattle about Sissy's coming back, that I grew a little home-sick and looked wistfully into grandmamma's face as she read the letter. This would always make her say: "You don't want to go home, little one? Aren't you very happy here with Lottie and the boys? And you are getting on so nicely with your books, too; mamma is so pleased to have you with so many little schoolfellows, and kind Miss Grant to teach you! And we are going to have all kinds of pleasant treats in the holidays. No, no, we must keep you another month or two! Perhaps we will send you home when the cold weather comes!" So I ran away again to make plans with Lottie about all the many things that must be done the very first day of no lessons.

Then came the last time of history, and the last dreadful sums, and the last copy written, and the last hard French words learnt, and then, happiest of all, the last putting away of books and cleaning of slates! It almost makes me take that long breath for joy even now only to remember that happy day.

"And don't you think I'm the happiest of us all?" said Miss Grant; "I am the only one really going home for the holidays!"

Which remark was a great relief to my little mind, for I had been afraid we must seem a great deal too glad that she was going. Now I could venture on my very loudest "hurrah," which, after all, was but a feeble imitation of the boys' loud cheers.

You know, anticipation is the best part of every pleasure; in easier words, everything looks brighter before it comes than when it *is* come. I think that was very nearly the happiest day of my whole year at Beecham, when I sat on the floor watching the last things put into Miss Grant's box, and chattering away about the happy days coming. You see, for a long time I had got up every morning with the thought of how many good marks I should get, and of how those hard letters and figures were to be made, and though I had made many a brave fight and won many a delightful victory over the books, yet it *was* very nice to think that to-morrow I should awake with the holiday feeling instead.

And the next morning did really come, though we thought it never would, and we made a very long meal of breakfast, being not quite sure what was to come next.

It was a funny day, that first day! Grandmamma and Uncle Hugh went away early for a long drive, and all sorts of business at the end of it; and we knew they would not be home till ever so late. It was very hot— oh, so *very* hot! We could not go into the sun at all, but Susette and Jane sent us out of the nursery very soon, that we might not disturb baby's midday sleep by our holiday fun. The school-room, of course, we avoided; so, after a little hesitation, we went out into the shade to play.

And, first of all, we thought of the swing as the best thing to be done, and for half an hour it *was* most delightful! Don't you know the pleasant feeling it is, just up at the very highest point, when you are not *quite* sure whether you are frightened or not? Don't you know? And you laugh a little anxiously, and are very glad to find yourself safely down again. Oh, it was very good fun for *a little while!* Only Harry came to swing us, and he was so fond of seeing your feet up into the branches, that you never could be quite sure that he would not send you head-over-heels. Lottie was very brave, but I could not quite stand it, so I stood by and watched; and when they asked me to have another try, I said, "No, thank you." I think Alick saw that I was a little red and uncomfortable, for he asked me to come and play on the lawn. We ran away, taking a last look at the two elder ones. It was not such boisterous play that we had, we two together, yet I think we enjoyed it very much, half-talking, half-playing. We were very good friends, and the morning went very quickly. When the dinner-bell rang, we agreed that we would start off together as soon as we could for the apple-orchard at the top of the hill, where we were not likely to be disturbed.

UP TO THE MOON!

That hot July afternoon, how well I remember it! All among the long grass we lay, looking up at the little, young apples overhead, and now and then setting our teeth in the sour middles of those that had fallen. But we were a little afraid of the effects of these unripe, bullet things, so we did no more than taste them. Then my eight-year-old cousin began to say me long pages of poetry, and when he had exhausted his stores, he astonished me by the funny, learned sound of his Latin declensions.

"You know, Sissy," he said, "I mean to be a very learned man some day, and know twelve or fourteen languages, I think. I shall not be content till I know more than anybody else. It will be nice to be wiser than papa. He's ever so clever, you see; but then, of course, new things will be found out every year, and sons must always get a-head of their fathers, or else the world would stand still, you see."

I didn't quite see, but I pretended to. Alick had been very confidential lately, and I knew what a sore spot there was in his heart making him talk like this. Hadn't he confided to me with a fierce, red heat on his forehead how his father had told him he wasn't "half a boy," because he had turned giddy climbing a high tree? "But papa always says when Harry bangs his head about, that he doesn't believe there can be any brains behind such a skull as his. I dare say that is the difference between us."

So said the young scholar with all the satisfaction possible, and I believed in him with all my heart.

HOLIDAY TIME

However, even he grew tired of wise talk, and proposed
a game with the fallen apples. How we pelted each
other, how we laughed, and, oh, how hot we did get at
last! Then off came hats and jackets, and were left
behind under the trees while we went to rest ourselves
in a piece of open shade, thrown by that large barn
where, by and by, the apples would be stored away; and
this was the moment which I seized to get his advice
as to a new toy I had lately bought to send to Bobbie.
It was one of those wooden soldiers whose arms and
legs are to go by means of a string; but the string, you
know, is always getting hitched. This was the case
now, and it tasked all Alick's wonderful brains to set
it right. How my back and arm did ache as I held it up
for him, lying flat on the grass, to twitch, and pull,
and contrive, and, at last, to conquer! That happy
moment had just come when there was a sound of
wheels in the road near us. One minute more, and
Uncle Hugh's voice was heard calling us, and the

carriage stopped to take us up. What grand, glorious news we were told as we drove home, two hatless, jacketless, sun-burnt children, I must not tell you this time.

8

THE COTTAGE ON THE CLIFF

"Well, my dearie," said grandmamma, "uncle and I have just taken such a pretty little cottage for you all, high up on the cliff, looking right over the blue sea. And you are to go off and try if the fresh wind up there will put a little more colour into those cheeks of yours!"

My dear little friends, I had just nestled down snugly enough on grandmamma's silk dress and black lace shawl, never having the least idea of the dear, kind purpose of that long sixteen miles' drive, so you won't be surprised to hear that the news gave me such a start that I very nearly jumped out of the carriage. And Alick—well, I don't know whether he was really half a boy or three quarters, but his shout certainly made you fancy him quite a *whole* boy at that minute!

Oh, the bright, bright pictures that came tumbling one over another in one's mind, at the idea of the cottage on the cliff, crabs and shrimps and shells and sea-weed, and merry, merry waves in one happy muddle! And do you know, nothing could induce the horses to trot fast enough up the long drive; they never seemed to consider one bit how much we had to tell, nor, indeed, how much we had *to do*, in preparation for to-morrow. What if they had done a good thirty miles since breakfast, they could stay at home next day and eat hay from morning to night and leave it to Fairy and Whitefoot to do the hot work for us.

I really cannot tell you how much sleep we got that night. I have a distinct remembrance of kicking all the bed-clothes off ever so many times, and of calling out to Lottie in the next room, without the smallest respect to rules. And there was Jane as busy as could be, with Susette, packing up little frocks, and pinafores, and nightgowns. Every now and then she would stop to say, "Really, Miss Sissy, you *must* be quiet, and go to sleep!" But, you know, that was just one of those remarks which it is of no use listening to.

It's funny how sometimes sleep seems to run away and won't be caught anyhow! Next night it was just the same. Only it was quite different, too. You know what I mean. That funny bedroom, with its white curtains covered with pink rose-buds, and the venetian blinds, and the moon shining through, mixed up somehow with the sound of the waves; and to have Lottie in the same large bed with me—oh, it was all so odd! And the narrow passages with two stairs at every turn, and the rooms opening right in each other's faces, so to say! It felt queer, too, to know that we were alone in the house with only Susette and Jane to

take care of us, the woman of the house to do hard
work, and Gus to run errands for us.

By some means or other we did go to sleep at last, and
afterwards woke up in the morning to wonder where
we were. And then came all the wonders of the new
place to be discovered. Harry had persuaded
grandmamma to send over the steady old pony with
us, and no sooner was breakfast over than he appeared
at the door led by Gus, for Master Harry to go, as he
called it, on a voyage of discovery. I am not sure that
our nurses were not rather glad to be rid of this "Turk
of a boy," as they called him; for Harry, good-natured
as he was, could not lose a chance of teasing the little
ones, and sometimes, a little hurting their tempers.

I'M COMING!

There was a great hollow place in the cliff close to our
house, down which was the way to the beach, which

we took with the least possible delay. Then came the first delights of bathing, and when that was over, the digging in the sand and hunting for shells, while baby took his morning sleep on Susette's lap. By and by we went home to dinner, and after that, to hemming and sewing and reading with the nurses. And when early tea was over, it was cool enough for a fresh walk over the hills, or away to the rocks farther off.

This was the way we spent four pleasant weeks, getting as rosy and strong as any one could wish. Three or four times we were surprised in our morning play on the beach by the welcome sight of Uncle Hugh. For, every now and then, he would ride over to give grandmamma some news of the children. This was a great delight, for it was sure to mean, first of all, that there were letters from home for us all,— those foreign sheets that Lottie loved to see, and the long crossed letters full of mamma's love to me. And to us four elder ones, Harry and Lottie and Alick and me, uncle's visit always meant a glorious afternoon in a boat far out at sea. I hardly know whether Harry or Gus delighted most in the prospect of these visits. The pleasure simply of holding the "Capitaine's" horse was enough to make the French boy's eyes glisten and his teeth shine with the broadest smile. And to Harry the delight of handling an oar or managing a sail was beyond anything delicious.

But the visit which we had all most cause to remember was the last which Uncle Hugh paid us. He was going away to London on business—business which would soon end in another long voyage, the news of which brought a flush of pleasure to Gus's cheeks, soon changed to intense disappointment at the news that he must this time be left in England.

That afternoon we were longer than usual on the sea, only returning just in time for a late tea and bed. Uncle Hugh started about seven o'clock, and Harry as usual mounted his pony in great haste to go with him part of the way. I remember that uncle was in a hurry, and did not wait for him, for as I stood undressing near the window I saw Harry waving his hat and calling after him, with the two dogs at his side.

THROUGH THICK AND THIN

The long summer evening faded away; from my pillow

I saw the stars come out one by one, and then kissing my hand to them, I let my sleepy eyes go shut, and was soon in the midst of pleasant dreamland. I don't know how long after this it was, that I was aroused by a sound of whispers at the door, and then by a little timid question from Lottie, "Susette, isn't Harry come home?" "But no, Miss Lottie," was the answer in a troubled voice, and Jane broke in: "Hush, hush! you'll wake Miss Sissy! Go to sleep, there's a darling. He'll be home directly now—no need to be frightened!"

"No need to be frightened!" said Susette, in her foreign accent. "But, yes——"

Jane had pulled her out of the room, and Lottie and I, now wide awake, were left to wonder, and talk in low, frightened tones. Lottie had heard the whining of one of the dogs under the window—both dogs had gone off with Harry—and she had heard Susette call Jane gently, and then they had whispered outside the door something about Gus and the dog; and after that she had heard Gus run off under the window, the dog barking joyfully and going, too. How we lay and trembled! By and by I got out of bed, and peeped through the Venetians, in spite of Lottie's entreaties.

"Oh, Sissy, please don't! Susette will be so angry! Please, Sissy, come back!"

I protested that Susette was not *my* nurse, yet I knew she could scold in such a bewildering torrent of French as did sometimes frighten me; and as I could see nothing but the calm, beautiful starlit sky over the sleeping sea, I dropped the blind, and sprang back into bed. It made a noise as I dropped it, and for some time the fear of being heard, and the anxiety to appear asleep if any one came, made us forget our alarm about Harry. In fact, I think we were getting sleepy again—I was, at least—but we started up at the sound of the hall-door softly opened, and then men's footsteps on the stairs. There was a low moan as the steps passed our door. Oh, how breathlessly we waited! Once, even, I had the door ajar, and was peeping out, when a hurried hand outside suddenly shut it again, making me start back. By and by there was a sound of footsteps going downstairs, and in a moment Lottie and I were both in the passage entreating Jane to tell us what had happened.

"Master Harry has been tumbled over the pony's head, Miss Lottie," she said, "and he's been lying in a ditch nobody knows how long; but the dog's saved his life—him and Gus together—and the doctor hopes he won't be very bad, no bones being broken, only bruises and knocks of the head. He don't quite know himself, you see, yet, poor young gentleman! and we have to keep him quiet, so you must go and be as still as mice. The doctor'll be here in the morning, and the missis, too, may be!"

All this while she was tucking us into bed again, and when she drew the curtains and left us we were afraid to whisper even, for fear of being heard in the next room and hurting Harry.

At breakfast the next morning we were told that Gus was "nigh about at Beecham by this time," and before evening the carriage had come just in sight, and stopped, and grandmamma was walking up to the house.

Then followed a very quiet week, during which we never spoke aloud without getting a sharp "hush!" Indeed, we were not allowed to be in the house a minute longer than necessary, being down on the beach whenever we were not eating, drinking, or sleeping. By the end of the week, Harry was to be seen at these rare intervals looking very pale, and quiet, and unlike himself on the sofa. I distinctly remember feeling rather pleased as I looked from him to Alick, and thought how much more of a boy Alick looked with his brown, rosy face, than the pale, languid, almost girlish elder brother, speaking in a weak, tired voice from his pillow. It was about another ten days before the close carriage came from Beecham, and with plenty of soft cushions, Harry was laid in it, and driven away back to the Park.

When we saw him there on our return, he was almost himself again, merry and bright, but a little pale and easily tired.

9

SUSETTE AND HER TROUBLES

So we all came back to Beecham Park, and the holidays were over, and we had to buckle to work again; work that had a pleasant mixture of play in it, out-of-door fun, Saturday rambles and birthday treats.

When first we returned from the sea-side there came a very earnest letter from mamma, begging that Sissy might really be sent home now, for surely grandmamma had had enough, and too much, of her. Indeed, a message was added at the end to say that papa had made up his mind to take a holiday and run down to fetch me. All seemed to be settled, and I myself got into that doubtful state—glad to go home but, oh, so sorry to leave this happy Beecham home! I began to wonder, too, whether I should feel quite at home with papa when he came, and on the morning fixed for his arrival, a very shy fit came over me, so that, at first, it seemed rather a relief when Harry called out to me that a letter had come from my home, and that I was to go up to grandmother at once. But what a grave, sad face met me! My very heart stood still as she kissed me. Then in gentle words she told me that Bobbie was ill, had caught the scarlet fever, so papa could not come.

And, to dear grandmamma, I think it was a very anxious time that followed. My little head could not take in all it meant when news came of danger, then of baby's illness, then of nurse's. I could see that other people were sorry; once I found Jane crying, and was caught up on to her lap and kissed and talked to, till a clear memory of the dear, chubby little brother at home came back to me, and I had a long, miserable fit of sobbing. But, you see, I had been away from them all for nearly six months, and the little brothers and sisters around me had somehow shut out the two little fellows at home, and my play and lessons at Beecham seemed much more real than the sorrow all those miles away. In a few weeks all the worst time was over, but, of course, there was no idea now of my going home.

I wonder if grandmamma ever thought, in the early spring, that for a whole year she was to have her house full of children! For a long time we fancied every week that we should hear of aunt and uncle coming home. Every now and then Lottie and I would fret a little bit at the idea of parting, but still it did not come.

One morning brought a letter for Lottie, with a great deal of news in it. She read it to me in the nursery, as we were having our hair brushed for the evening in the drawing-room. It told us that her papa had just made up his mind to take the work of a clergyman in a more out-of-the-way part, somewhere between

Switzerland and Germany, and that it was just the place to suit her mamma, so they would probably stay there till Christmas. Besides, there were some little German cousins of Lottie's living close by with their aunt, so there was a great deal to tell altogether. We were very eager talking about little Heinrich and Carl—so eager that at first we never noticed that Susette had thrown herself into a chair with clasped hands, and her black eyes full of tears. When we came to question her, she said Monsieur and Madame had gone to a place close to her native village, and would they—oh, would they—see her poor, poor father, in the misery extreme, frightful! We were quite used to Susette now, and not at all surprised at her passionate manner; and if we did a little smile to each other at that favourite word "affreuse," yet Lottie was eager and sincere enough in her assurances that certainly papa would go and look for the poor family. Out came the foreign paper at once, and if the summons to the dining-room had not come at that moment, I believe the letter would have been written there and then. As it was, it certainly went the next day. It was our first piece of anything like charity, and we waited eagerly for the answer from Lottie's papa, which, of course, did not arrive directly it was wanted.

At last the morning came, when the postman, met by three eager children half-way down the drive, was greeted by the happy cry, "Oh, there it is! I see it in his hand!" And the much-longed-for prize was snatched from him, and triumphantly carried off to the nursery.

"Oh, children, do keep off! You must let Susette hear!"

cried Lottie, and then she read this. But first let me say that this wonderful letter, having been put away with other more important old papers, has become very worn and yellow, and you must forgive me if I leave out a piece here and there, where it is too torn to read.

"'My dear Lottie and all the Chicks,—Your letter came very safely all by itself the other day, just as well as if it had been in grandmamma's as usual; and papa knew what an eager little woman his Lottie was, and so he made his discoveries as soon as possible, and here they are! Poor Susette, I don't wonder she was anxious to know all about her poor father, and the rest of them. They have had a hard time of it since she left them, but they are all so fond of her, and so glad to get news of her. Such a good girl as she is to them all! Mind, children, you make much of her, and don't add to all she has to worry about."

At this point we all looked at Susette, and little Murray squeezed her hand. Her black eyes were overflowing, and her rosy lips were pressed tightly together; yet she was looking very happy and pleased.

Then Lottie went on:—

"'Heinrich and I set off at once to —' (reader, I *cannot* read the name of the village!), 'but some time before we got there we met a pretty Swiss girl, with a bundle of corn on her head, whose eyes and mouth reminded me very much of your kind nurse. So I put my hand on Heinrich's shoulder to stop him, and then I asked her if her name was Laurec, and she said, "Yes." So we

SUSETTE'S SISTER

had a long talk, and she told me all about them at
home, and of the fever in the village, and the want of
work, and all the rest. I fancy it has been little short
of starvation for them all this long time. Then I let
her hurry on to tell them at home who was coming.
Such a sweet hill-side village as I cannot hope to
make my little English birds understand, with its
pretty chalets lying against the rock, and the bushy
trees shooting out of the cliff above and around them.
I went up to the one pointed out to me, and there,
lying on a heap of rags, was Susette's little blind
sister, that she has often talked to you about. Dear
little patient thing! turning her large, dark, sightless

eyes towards me with such a bright smile! As she spoke of "le bon Dieu," I thought of the pretty French hymns you used to try to learn, and it gave the soft French words a softer sound when they were on such a happy theme. But we could not stay there; so making our little present to the dear child, we set off up the mountain. We had not gone far, when, among a flock of goats scattered over the hill, we found a poor old man sitting on a rock, with very downcast look, and little Pierre Laurec, who had come to show us the way, told us it was his father. The poor old man was very much out of heart, and it was some time before we could make him understand that we wanted to help him. At Susette's name he looked mournfully in my face as I sat down by him, murmuring that she was gone, gone, bonne fille!

UNHAPPY

"'Well, you know, I must not make my letter too long. Tell Susette that things look brighter now in her old home; that Pierre has found some work in our garden, and his sister comes now and then to your aunt's house; and that we will look after them a little, and send you more news soon.

"'Mamma sends ever so much love, and many, many thanks to dear grandmamma for offering to house her tiresome chicks for a few more months. What a grand, happy Christmas we will have together! That is, if only I can get mamma well enough to brave an English winter. Poor mamma wants sadly to get a sight of her baby.—Ever your affectionate

"'Father.'"

That was the letter, reader. Don't you think it was well worth waiting for?

10

AUTUMN DAYS

"What an idea, papa talking about Christmas!" Alick said, when we came to the end of the letter; and it did seem funny that hot autumn afternoon, when all the leaves were in a glow, looking as if they had been burnt up so long they couldn't and wouldn't bear it any longer! Perhaps they meant to come down. But I suppose, now I come to think of it, that months don't seem so never-ending to grown-up people as they do to children; they are more prepared to see the time fly, you don't know how, so they are not surprised when they find it gone. Besides, you see, they don't get taller and taller as the months pass, so, of course, the time must seem to run past very quickly, they standing still all the while! How odd it must be! I heard a little boy remonstrating last night—

"Well, but, uncle, if you keep your clothes till next year they'll be ever so much too small for you!"

Everybody laughed, and told him that uncle, being six feet high, didn't expect to grow any more; and, of course, as I said before, if Alick's papa stood still, the time *would* seem to go very quickly.

And so, I suppose, when the end of October came, he didn't cry out as we did all of a sudden: "I do declare it is not quite two months to Christmas!"

It was one damp, misty afternoon, and Lottie, and Alick, and I were learning our lessons all alone in the school-room. We were trying to get the last glimmer of daylight at the window, but it was hardly enough to see what six times nine might be, and that was my great difficulty.

You know, don't you? how the things that "you do so want to say" will come into your head just when you ought to be very silent and busy! It's *very* odd; but even now that I am old enough to know better, I never want so much to talk as just when I ought to be quiet. I wonder how it is? Anyhow, it seemed quite impossible to hold one's tongue that afternoon. Alick was as busy and quiet as could be, working out a hard sum on his slate, but even he looked up when Lottie started that wonderful idea about Christmas; and then we all joined in wondering how the time had gone, and what lots of fun Christmas would bring with it. I had my own particular share of delight, for was there not a certain prospect of papa and mamma coming to the Park to take me home? My little cousins, too, were looking forward to home directly after Christmas; but their mamma could not come and fetch them. She had been well enough to travel, and would be in England very soon now; that is, in the little island down in the south, you know, where the invalids go.

She would get a nice home ready for them there and then, as she said in her letters, "have the delight of calling back all the chicks under her wings again!"

Well, it was just all these things that we were talking about over our lesson-books at the school-room, when our attention was caught by two figures coming up the drive in the mist. Such a foggy afternoon as it was, all the dead leaves hanging yellow and dripping from the trees! It was not till they got quite up to the house that we saw that the two men were going to give us some music. One had some bagpipes and the other a kind of horn, and, of course, all thought of lessons went out of our heads when we heard them begin. What fun it was to listen, and to watch their queer grimaces and antics, as they danced about to their own music!

But we had not been enjoying this long when a terrible thing happened. Oh, little reader, it makes me shudder now!

You must understand that our school-room was on the ground-floor, but raised a good way from the ground; a separate room built out from the house, the roof sloping out under the windows of the day-nursery.

The first thing we thought of was calling the little ones to hear the music; but when I proposed it, Alick said he was sure they knew all about it, he could hear their voices. Lottie declared that that was impossible; we never heard anything from the nursery unless the window was open. Just then the men began to beg, and Alick ran off to get some pence. Grandmamma said

they were to have a cup of the servants' tea, and Alick
went to the kitchen to ask for it. When he came back,
he told us that Susette was down there getting baby's
supper, and that Jane was teazing her about her
"brothers the players!"

GIVE US A COPPER!

"Oh, Alick!" cried Lottie, "then that's it! Murray and
Bertie have got the window open to hear better, and in
all this fog and wet!"

Alick was just going to laugh at her for being such an

"old fidget," when we were startled by a loud cry, and the sound of something falling down the roof. At the same moment we saw Harry rushing up to the house—he was just home from his lessons at the curate's—throwing his arms about in the most excited way.

"Oh, it's Murray tumbled out of window?" cried Lottie. And away we all rushed to the front door, feeling sick with fear.

Now, up the side of the wall grew a very thick, bushy fig-tree, the stem of which was very big of its kind. When we rushed out into the foggy air, there was Harry clambering so cleverly up among the large, wet leaves; and on the edge of the roof, caught by his clothes in some way that we could not see, was poor little Murray! Susette covered her face with her hands, and most of us turned away too frightened to look. I remember hiding my face in Jane's gown, and feeling her stroking my hair; and I never looked up till there was a cry that it was all right, and Harry and Murray were both safe on the ground again.

How glad we all were, and how we all talked at once, and said how we had felt, and how Murray cried though he wasn't hurt, only frightened—all this I mustn't stop to tell you. By and by it came to be one of those things that are always nice to talk about with shudders, and sighs, and laughter. Many and many a tea-time the same wonder and thankfulness were repeated, always beginning with, "Don't you remember that dreadful day?" and so on.

Meanwhile Christmas was coming, and Christmas

weather came sooner still. Then the snow collected outside the nursery window, and the mornings were very dark, and bed the only comfortable place; and Gus's hands got blue, and his face thin and pinched, and he wished himself away with the "Capitaine" in the warm South Seas.

LOOK AT ME!

But there was fun, too, about that cold weather; fun with the snow-man in the Park; fun in learning to skate on the frozen pond, shut in so nicely with the fir-trees; and fun in the real Christmas treats, Christmas-trees, and Christmas games.

And so it was a very bright time that came to finish up those happy Beecham days. The end of it all was saying "good-bye" to grandmamma and cousins one fine, frosty morning, just the other side of New Year's Day, and driving off between papa and mamma.

When you think of my first evening in that drawing-room, perhaps you will wonder at the doubtful look which I know there was on my face, and which made papa look right into my eyes, questioning, as he said,

"Whether I wanted to go home or not."

11

GOOD-BYE TO BEECHAM

Was I glad to go home or sorry? How could I tell? When it came to the train, it was all such fun that I chattered away to mamma as fast as possible about the stations we should pass, and the things we should see, till I saw an old gentleman opposite exchanging smiles with mamma. That made me feel shy, and shrink back into the corner silent enough; and with the silence came a sigh, and five minutes later mamma's question surprised me, in a fit of melancholy thought, about all that I had left behind me. When would Lottie and I meet again? And how should we know which was getting on best with the history? Ah, those nice history lessons, with all those exciting stories and our favourite heroes, who would read them with me now? I am not at all sure that I did not have to choke down two or three tears before I could answer mamma. Do you think she noticed it?

We were getting near our own station now, and I grew very eager, looking out for papa's brougham. How cold the air was, going out of the station, and what a cosy remembrance of home feeling there was about the soft corner, where I had often nestled when driving with papa!

I don't remember much about Bobby's welcome; I know both little brothers seemed a little strange to me till about the middle of tea-time. Bobby was very hot and excited with his half-hour before the nursery fire, making toast for Sissy's first tea at home. I could feel that he was looking at me very hard, but I don't think we were either of us quite comfortable till he had thrown his arms round my neck, repeating his old cry, "Nursey, I'm so glad Sissy's come home!" After that it was all right, and we chattered away nineteen to the dozen. Dear old nurse! she was as pleased to see me again as possible. Indeed, I am not sure that she did not keep me up half an hour later than mamma intended, just talking to me and "blessing my little heart," in her own loving fashion. When I went through the night nursery at last to my own little room, I made her let me stop and look at the little ones; and what a hugging and kissing she gave me when I declared that they were ever so much prettier than the Beecham cousins. Dear little Bobby, with his sweet, rosy, budding mouth, and baby Willie's round cheeks and bright, golden curls, I can remember just how they looked!

In a day or two we settled down together, and I was quite at home. The only person who still seemed restless was Jane. For two or three weeks she was always talking about the Park, and wishing herself back there. Then, all of a sudden, she grew quite bright and happy, and talked away to nurse in quite a different way.

I didn't know what it all meant; and especially, I couldn't think why she was always getting so red when nurse talked about flowers and plants. At last I found out that Jane was going away altogether; and a month or two after Christmas, nurse dressed Bobby and me one day, and took us to church, and mamma took care of baby at home. And at church we saw Jane with her father and mother, and I whispered to Bobby that the strange man with them was Mr. Owen, grandmamma's head-gardener, and I couldn't think how he came to be in our church! But when the service was all over, nurse took us into the vestry, and told us to go and give Jane a kiss, because she was Mrs. Owen now, and we must "say something pretty."

It doesn't seem to do to tell little folks that sort of thing. You remember, when Jane herself gave me that charge ever so long ago, it didn't answer, and now there was Bobby crying and sobbing out that "Mr. Owen shouldn't take Janie away; he was a naughty man; he didn't like him at all!" But nobody seemed to mind this, indeed they all looked pleased; and Mr. Owen turned round, and asked me if he should take me back to Beecham too?

Ah, by this time, I was quite sure, and didn't hesitate at all when I said, "No, thank you, I'd rather stay at home."

And now, little readers, I meant to have tumbled you off my knee, and sent you up to bed, for I fancy my story has not kept you from getting sleepy. But there is nursie making signs to me, as much as to say, "Go on talking; amuse the little ones a bit longer, please, for the bath isn't ready and the water isn't hot, and I can't have them yet."

What shall I tell you about? Oh, I know! that second visit of mine to Beecham. It was only a very short one, so five minutes' talk will tell you all about it.

I was a great tall girl then, and I had just left school, when grandmamma's letter came, asking Bobby and me to come and spend a few days at the Park with Lottie, and Harry, and Alick. I couldn't say, "No, thank you," if I had wished to, for it was likely to be the last time we five should meet for a long time. Harry, now a young lieutenant with brass buttons and fair moustache, was bound on a long voyage, which would have some fighting at the end; and Lottie was to be married in a fortnight, and to go off to Australia; and Alick, too, was just starting on a tour with his tutor, after which he was to go to a great college in Germany. But there was another reason for our visit which I did not know till I got there, though, I fancy, mamma did. Grandmamma met us with a very tearful welcome, and it was natural for us all to feel sad as we looked at her, so aged since we saw her last, and in her deep, deep mourning. We couldn't help thinking of the blue sea far away, with the soft spicy wind blowing from the beautiful coral islands over the quiet waves, which had so cruelly sucked in dear Uncle Hugh's brave ship and all on board. But the pleasure of meeting soon put away all sad thoughts, and I think even grandmamma looked bright and contented as she listened to our merry talk.

It was in the middle of the long summer days, and we

rambled about through the gardens, and orchards, and shrubberies where we had played as little children, and laughed over the remembrance of our childish tricks and troubles. Then there was that long talk with grandmamma, and afterwards with Bobby, in her room. When Lottie and I found ourselves alone together just at bed-time, how much we had to say! It seemed to me a little difficult to talk over all her affairs, though when, after some time, she called upon me to admire my two tall cousins, I was quite ready to do so. Yet my own rosy, round-faced, romping schoolboy brother was much more in my thoughts now.

I don't think I had ever known till now that my mother was grandmamma's eldest child, so it had never struck me that, now that dear uncle was gone, Bobby, and not Harry, would be master of Beecham Park! How strange it did seem! I thought of the funny boy's blushing awkwardness when grandmamma had told him, and then of his confession to me that "it was a horrid bore, he had so meant to be a discoverer, and get lost in Africa like Dr. Livingstone; and now, he supposed, he couldn't!" And just before I went to sleep that night I thought of his last words about it a few hours ago, as he threw his strong arm over my shoulder:—

"I say, Sis, it'll be ever so long first—that's one comfort!—but if ever I do have to come and live here, you'll come too, won't you? Then you can see after it all, you know, and then it won't be quite so bad!"

Should I? Would Beecham ever be my real home? And

Jane—Jane down at the Lodge with her three rosy, tidy little daughters. Wasn't this just what she said years ago when she first brought me to Beecham? "What if Master Bobby should grow up some day to find it all his own, and he the lord of it all!"

So it had come to pass, and Beecham, dear beautiful Beecham, was to be really *ours*!

That was a dozen years ago, my small friends; how funny it seems now!

THE END

www.ingramcontent.com/pod-product-compliance
Lightning Source LLC
Chambersburg PA
CBHW020644130626
46552CB00003B/1389